LETTUCE
PUMPKIN
SWISS

THE CHILDREN'S GARDEN

Growing Food in the City

CAROLE LEXA SCHAEFER *Illustrated by* PIERR MORGAN

Manufactured in China by C&C Offset Printing Co. Ltd.
Shenzhen, Guangdong Province, in December 2016

Published by Little Bigfoot, an imprint of Sasquatch Books
21 20 19 18 17   9 8 7 6 5 4 3 2 1

Editors: Tegan Tigani, Christy Cox
Production editor: Emma Reh
Design: Anna Goldstein

Library of Congress Cataloging-in-Publication Data is available.

ISBN: 978-1-57061-984-7

Sasquatch Books
1904 Third Avenue, Suite 710
Seattle, WA 98101
(206) 467-4300
www.sasquatchbooks.com
custserv@sasquatchbooks.com

To Sage and William,
Paul, Ben, and Jorge—
and especially TEd—
for the TLC in my garden —C. L. S.

To Devin, who loves to dig in the dirt —P. M.

SUNNYSIDE

Down the road from Woodlawn Avenue, on a street called Sunnyside, there's a garden patch grown by children who live in the neighborhood.

A sign on the garden's gate says:

That means: Come in, please.

Listen, see, smell, touch—even taste!

In the Children's Garden, deep, dark soil—rich with rotted grass, apple peels, and onion skins—is tunneled through by worms who wriggle it loose and give it air—*ahhh*.

In the Children's Garden, well-worn tools, rows
of spades, rakes, and hoes are used—

sca-ritch, sca-rutch—to turn, to pile, to dig in the soil, making mounds and holes.

In the Children's Garden, all sorts of seeds—round brown, plump white, flat black—are scattered or

dropped

one

by

one,

then covered by hands that pat, pat, pat.

In the Children's Garden, boxes, pots, and plots full of soil and seeds get soaked by showers from clouds or hoses, buckets or cans, so everything stays drip-drop damp—even under the sizzling sun.

PEPPER MINT
CHOCOLATE MINT
LEMON

In the Children's Garden, tender sprouts pop out of soft earthy beds, slim stemmed with leaves in twos—

all small—yet strong enough to stretch their green
tops up, and reach their root toes down.

In the Children's Garden, corn rows, strawberry clumps, lettuce groups, tomato clusters, sunflower stands, zucchini jumbles, and green bean tents grow, forming patterns that fill the spaces with leaves and flowers, vegetables and fruit.

In the Children's Garden, children call to each other:

"Listen to those crows caw and yack!"

"Well, talk back! Tell them to stay out of our corn."

“Look at the shape of this funny tomato.”

“Ha! It’s like a clown’s head with a big red nose!”

“Smell the peppermint I grew. Rub it with your fingers.”

“Mmm, I like to chew it.”

"Whew! Pulling weeds is hot, hard work."

“It’s cool inside the bean tent . . .”

"Let's take a rest."

In the Children's Garden, near the gate, dust-dappled children carrying brimful baskets home stop for a moment to watch while sunflowers do an evening dance, nodding their shaggy heads and rustling their leafy dresses.

On the gate, the sign still says:

Children's Garden WELCOME!

That means come back again with one friend or ten. And, if you like, in your own earth spot—a yard, a lot, or even a giant-size flowerpot—plant another children's garden.

Children's
Garden
WELCOME!

THE CHILDREN'S GARDEN IS A REAL PLACE.

It is located on Sunnyside Avenue in Seattle, Washington. I first wandered into it years ago on a summer evening walk. I knew right away that I wanted to write about this lively, lovely city garden tended by neighborhood children.

The garden was started by Seattle Tilth, an organization that helps people of all ages and means learn to grow their own food in an environmentally friendly way, and encourages people to eat locally and sustainably grown food. When Seattle Tilth (now called Tilth Alliance) began in 1978, members first broke asphalt to make a community learning garden at the Sunnyside location. Not long after, they created their first children's garden—the garden in this book.

Today, Tilth Alliance still manages this children's garden. They also manage another children's garden in South Seattle, as well as three regional community learning gardens and three educational farms. They offer school tours, mobile classrooms, and summer camps where children and youth learn about soil, critters, plants, growing food, and caring for the environment. They also offer many opportunities for adults—gardeners, farmers, and eaters.

As author of *The Children's Garden*, I want to acknowledge and thank Tilth Alliance. From seeds they planted, this book grew.

—Carole Lexa Schaefer

To learn more about Tilth Alliance and their programs for all ages, go to TilthAlliance.org.

CARROT
SUNFLOWER
UCCHINI
TOMATO
CORN